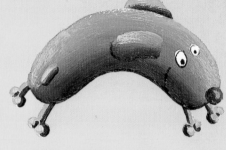
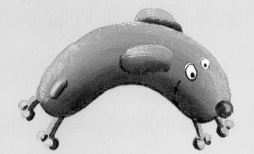

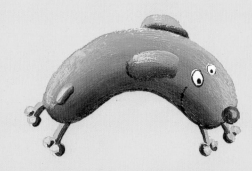
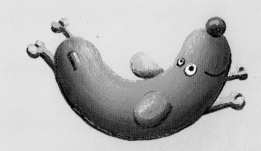

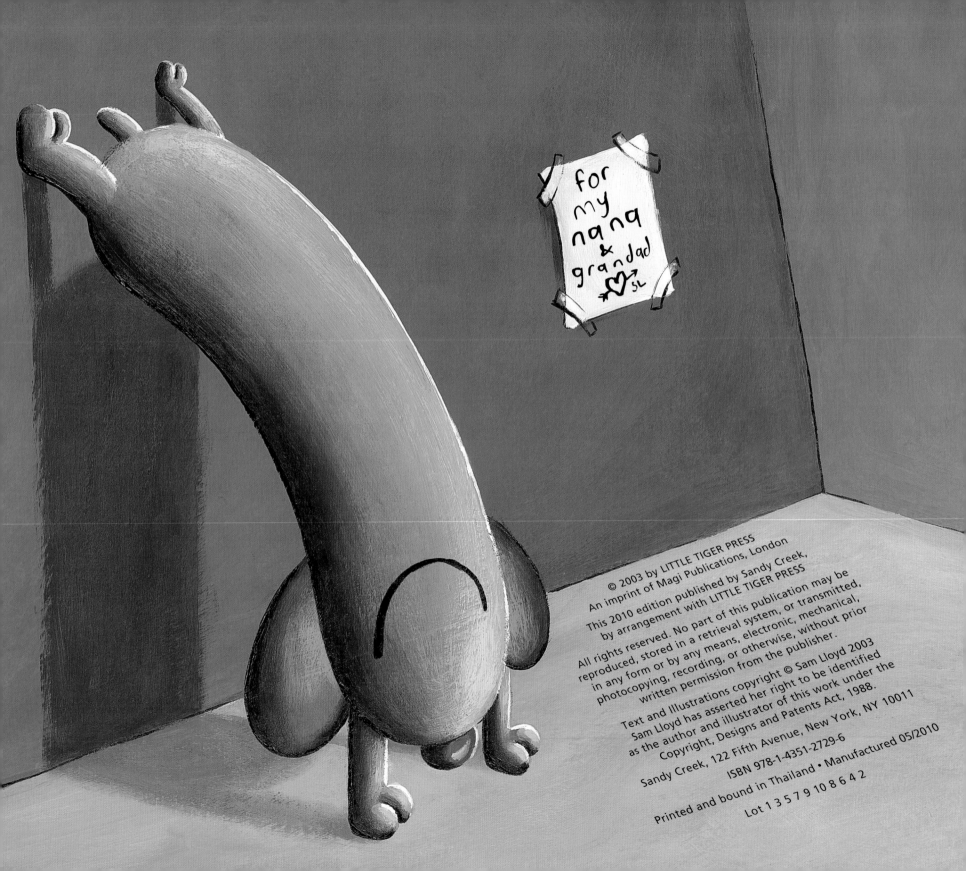

for
my
nana
&
grandad
SL

SUPER SID
THE SILLY SAUSAGE DOG

Sam Lloyd

Sid was a sausage dog who lived
in the shelter on the edge of town.
He lived there because he didn't have
a nice kind owner to love and care
for him like other dogs.

Sid wanted a nice kind owner more than anything. So he decided to find one for himself!

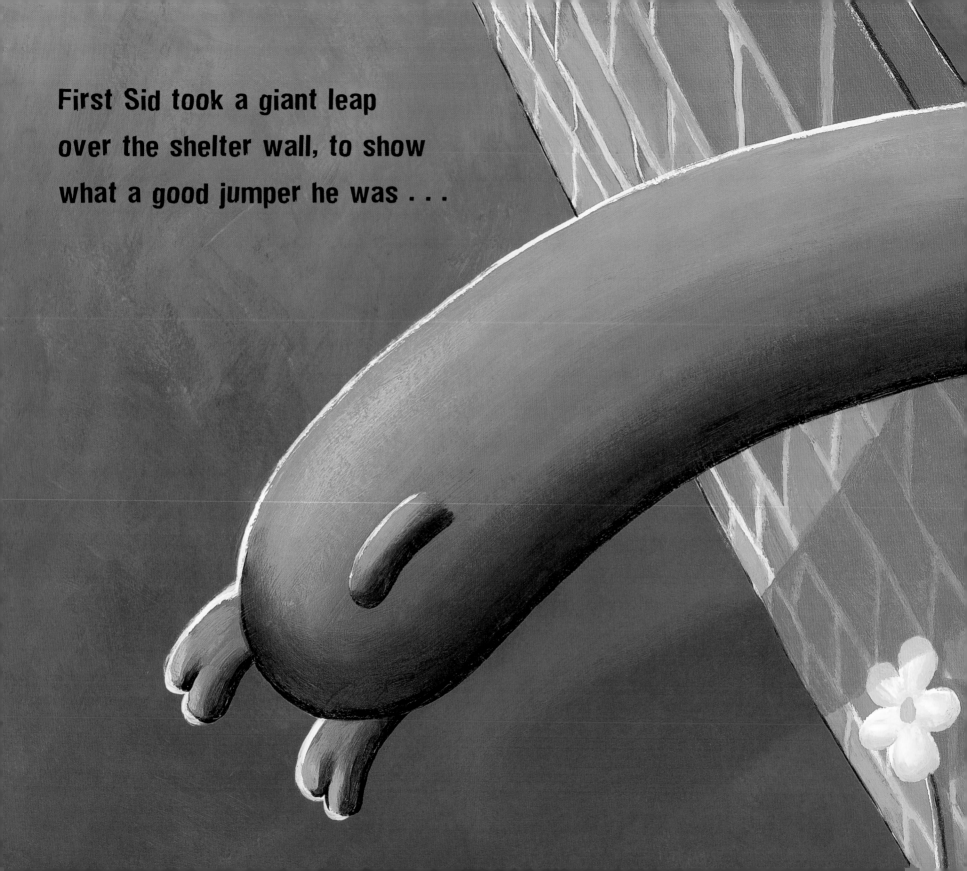

First Sid took a giant leap
over the shelter wall, to show
what a good jumper he was . . .

But . . .

. . . he landed on top of Madam Murples' very fancy afternoon party.

"Silly Sid!"
screeched the ladies.
"Back to the shelter
at once!"

Then Sid tried to show
everyone what a good
digger he was.

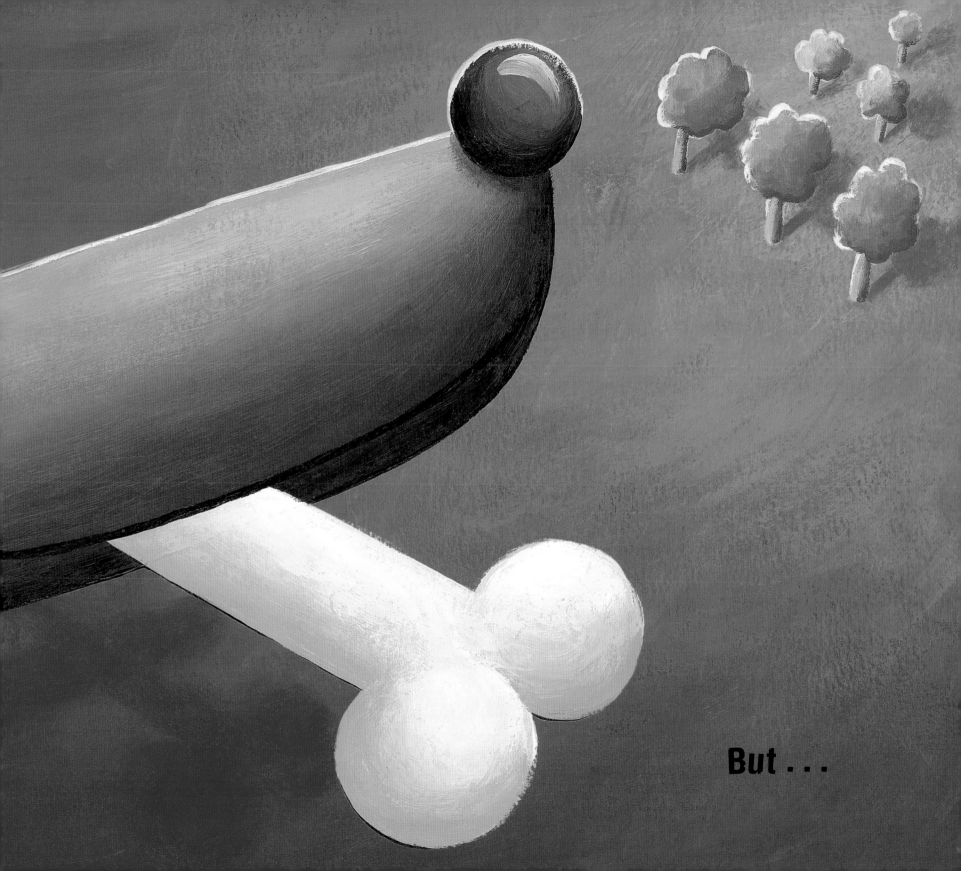

But . . .

. . . he dug up all Gardener Pete's prize vegetables.

"Silly Sid!" growled Pete. "Now I'll never win the best vegetable competition. Back to the shelter with you!"

"I know," thought Sid. "I'll show
everyone what a good singer I am.
That will cheer them up."
He howled and howled as loud as
his doggy lungs would let him.

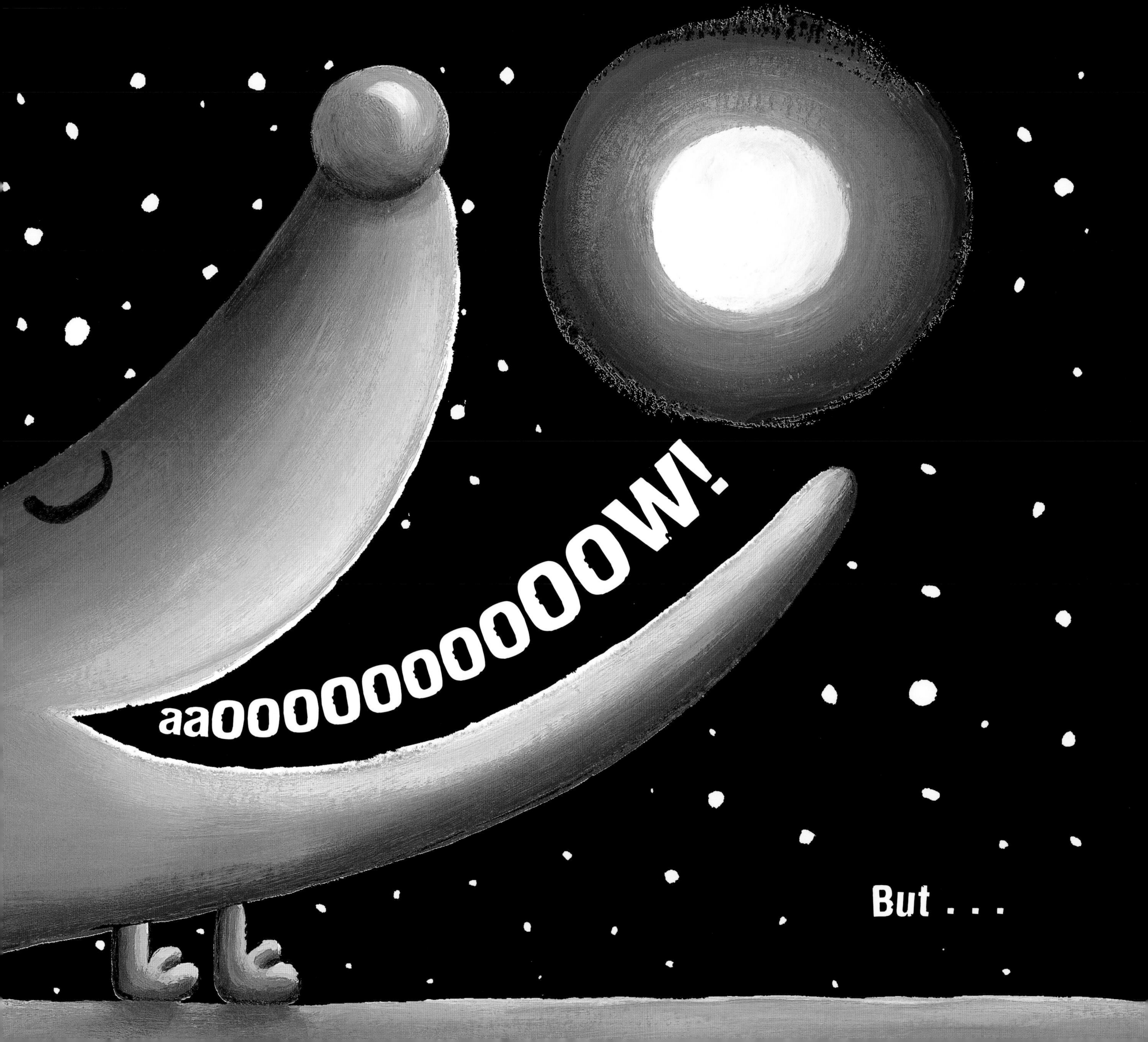

But . . .

. . . he woke the whole street!

"SILLY SID!"

they cried, throwing water at him.

"Go away!"

Poor Sid. Sad, wet and lonely
he crept back to the shelter.
"Nobody wants me," he thought.
"I'll never find a perfect home."

The next morning Sid was woken up by a very

strange smell. He put his nose into the air and, without thinking, he followed the smell . . . .

through the garden, around the bird table until at last he came to . . .

. . . A FIRE!

Little Billy's dinner was on fire.

Grandma had forgotten all about it.

aaOOOOOOOW!

Sid jumped up and down and he sang and he woofed. And he howled as loud as his doggy lungs would let him. Until . . .

. . . the fireman came and, with a rush and a gush and a great big splash, he put the fire out!

"Clever Sid," said Grandma.
"Brave Sid," said the fireman.
"Super Sid," said the crowd.

"My Sid!" said Little Billy.

So Sid had found not one but two of the nicest, kindest owners **ever!**

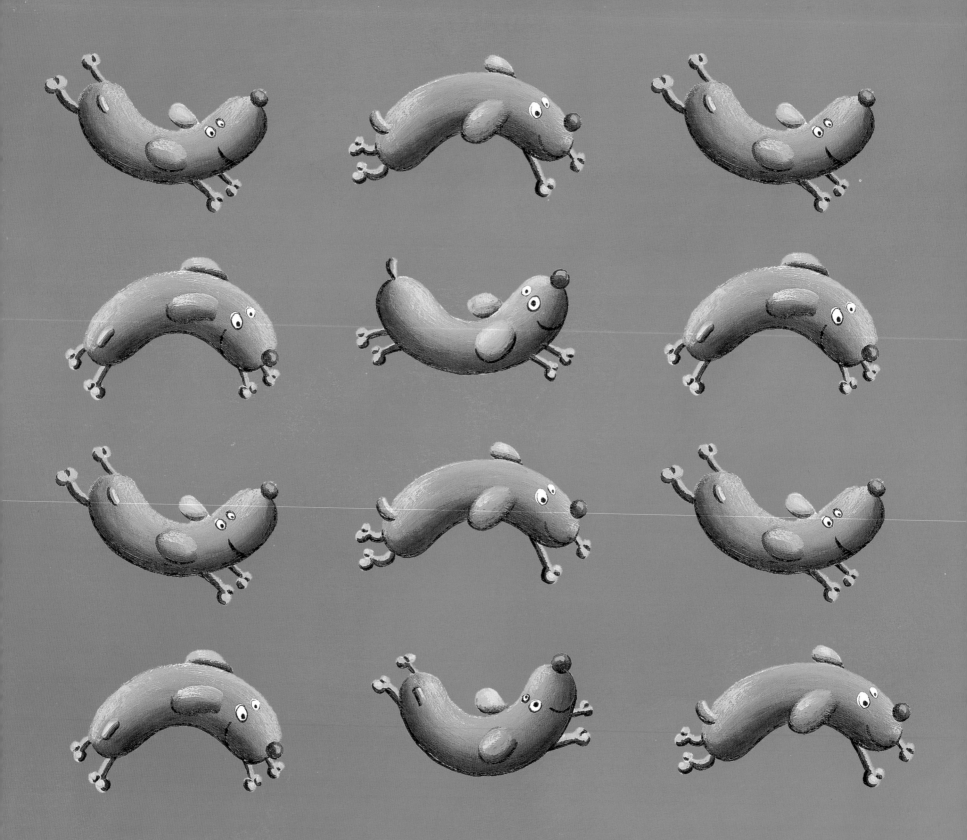